DONKEY NINA AND THE GIANT

STORY BY **John Carroll**

PICTURES BY **Sarah Chamberlain**

E. P. DUTTON   NEW YORK

Library of Congress Cataloging-in-Publication Data
Carroll, John, date
    Donkey Nina and the giant.
    Summary: Donkey Nina and her friend the snail set out
to protect the world from monsters.
    [1. Donkeys—Fiction.   2. Snails—Fiction.   3. Friendship
—Fiction]   I. Chamberlain, Sarah, ill.   II. Title.
PZ7.C234933Do   1989   [E]   88-33552
ISBN 0-525-44478-5

Published in the United States by E. P. Dutton,
a division of Penguin Books USA Inc.

Published simultaneously in Canada by
Fitzhenry & Whiteside Limited, Toronto

Designer: Riki Levinson

Printed in Hong Kong by South China Printing Co.
First Edition   10 9 8 7 6 5 4 3 2 1

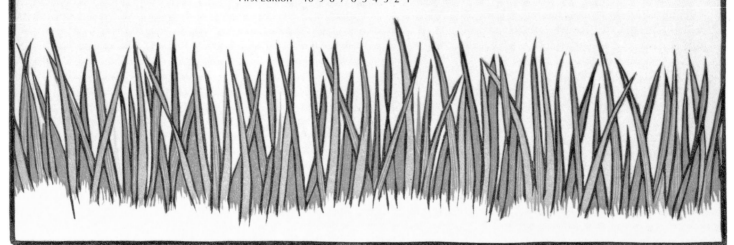

for Skylar and Jason
J.C.

for Jamie with love
and Donna with gratitude
S.C.

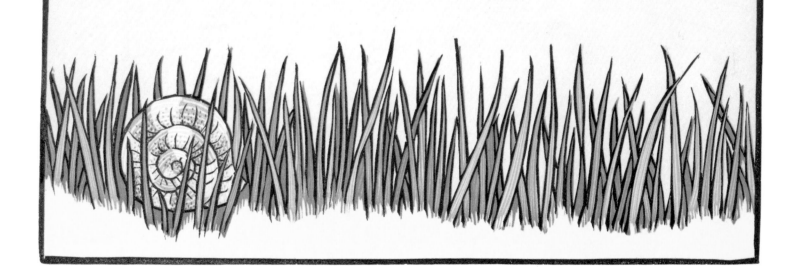

ne summer morning, Donkey Nina said good-bye
to her family. She kissed her mother and father and brother,
her aunt and uncle, and her grandmother and grandfather.

"I have something important to do," she said. "I am going
to protect the world. Good-bye, everyone."

She trotted off, singing to herself.

Soon she came to a very tall giant.

"Be off, giant," she said. "I am Donkey Nina. And I am protecting the world from monsters."

The giant did not move. The giant did not say a word.

"I am too little," said Donkey Nina, sadly. "I need someone to help me scare away the giant. I need a friend."

So off she went to find a friend.

"Hey! Watch where you're walking!"

Donkey Nina looked down. She saw a little snail. "Oh, I almost stepped on you."

"The story of my life," said the snail. "I'm always getting stepped on."

"I'm sorry," said Donkey Nina. "I was looking for a friend. I am Donkey Nina, and I am protecting the world from monsters. Can you help me scare away a giant?"

"How big is the giant?" the snail asked.

"Very, very big," replied Donkey Nina.

"I'm not afraid," said the snail. "Let's go."

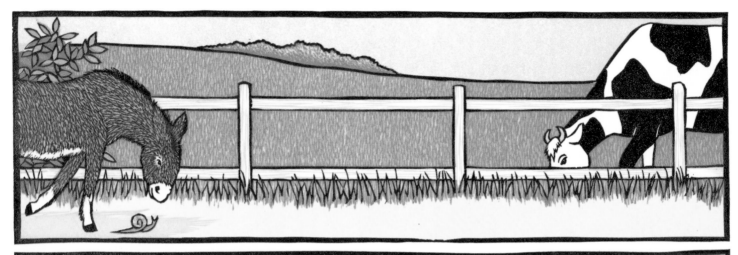

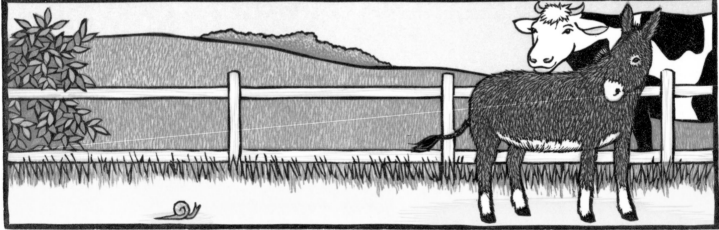

But there was a problem.
"Can't you move any faster?" said Donkey Nina.
"If you want to be my friend," said the snail, "you're going to have to be patient."

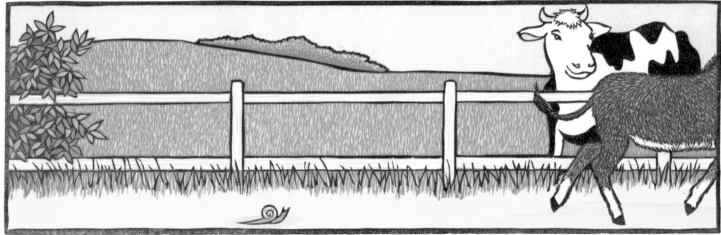

"You could ride on my back," Donkey Nina offered.

"If my friends saw me riding on a donkey's back, I'd never hear the end of it," said the snail.

"I'll find a wagon for you," said Donkey Nina.

Before long, Donkey Nina met a horse pulling a wagon full of hay.

"May I borrow your wagon?" asked Donkey Nina.

"No," said the horse.

"Please," said Donkey Nina.

"No," said the horse. "The farmer trusts me to get this hay to the barn. If I don't, he'd never trust me again. He wouldn't let me go out at night. I love to gallop in the dark. I love the sky when it's full of stars."

"I'll take the hay to the barn for you," said Donkey Nina. The horse thought for a while. "If I give you the wagon, then I can go off now. I've never galloped in the daylight when the sky is bright and empty."

The horse shook off his harness and galloped joyfully away.

Donkey Nina pulled the wagon along the path. Before she reached the barn, the wagon got stuck in the mud.
I'll ask the sun to dry up this mud, she thought.

She climbed a hill. "I need to be even closer to the sun, or it will never hear me. I need a ladder."
So Donkey Nina went off to find a ladder.

She looked and she looked.
But she couldn't find one anywhere.

I will have to build one, she thought.
First I must find some wood.

She came to a very tall tree.

"Here is the wood I need," she said.

"Would you chop me down?" asked the tree.

"I need a ladder to get near the sun," Donkey Nina replied. "I want to ask the sun to dry the mud. Then the wagon won't be stuck and I can take the hay to the barn. Then I can use the wagon to carry my friend the snail. And then we can . . . I forgot what we were going to do."

"Weren't you trying to scare away a giant?"

"Yes! You're right! I am protecting the world from monsters!"

The tree rustled. "Where is the giant?"

Donkey Nina tried to remember. So much had happened since she saw the giant. "This is very strange," she said at last. "I think I saw it here."

She stepped back from the tree. She looked up.

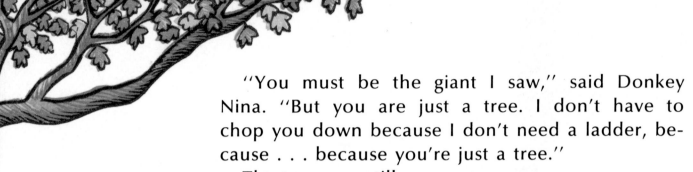

"You must be the giant I saw," said Donkey Nina. "But you are just a tree. I don't have to chop you down because I don't need a ladder, because . . . because you're just a tree."

The tree was still.

"Well, good-bye," said Donkey Nina. "You're a very beautiful tree."

Donkey Nina found the horse. He helped her pull the wagon out of the mud.

Then Donkey Nina took the wagon to the barn and said good-bye to the horse.

She went back to where she had left the snail.

"What took you so long?" the snail asked.

Donkey Nina told him what had happened. The snail was disappointed. "No giants? No adventure?"

"We could find another adventure," said Donkey Nina. "But we'll have to wait until tomorrow. It's getting late and I have to go home."

"That sounds nice," said the snail. "The only home I've got is on my back."

"Would you like to come home with me?" asked Donkey Nina. "You could meet my mother and father and brother, my aunt and uncle, and my grandmother and grandfather. And maybe you could spend the night and be my friend."

"Why not?" said the snail.

"You'll have to ride on my back," said Donkey Nina gently.

The snail thought for a moment. "I'll do it. But I'll have to hide. If another snail saw me, he'd call me lazy."

So the snail crawled onto Donkey Nina's back and hid in her fur. "If anyone asks," whispered the snail, "say I'm a burr. Burrs are very lazy."

Donkey Nina went home, and the snail stayed for dinner.

After dinner, the snail and Donkey Nina went to bed. They talked in the dark about monsters and giants. For a long time they were too frightened to sleep.

The next morning, the sun came up and nothing seemed
frightening anymore. So after breakfast they went off together
into the world.

And they protected it.